"What is it?" asked Robbie.

"It's a Beta fuel," Allen said. "It's used for long-range travel. Even small amounts can generate a lot of energy. But it's very unstable."

"What do you consider long-range?" asked Josh.

"Six to seven light-years," Allen said matter-of-factly. He continued to examine the substance.

"Is it from those Celuvians?" Robbie asked. "Maybe this is where they landed."

"No," Allen replied. "This is definitely Pontine. The Pontines are from the Nosyarg galaxy. Unlike the Celuvians, they are advanced. Very advanced." He looked around the clearing. "They've been here, but they're gone now."

"That makes two different alien species landing near Delport at around the same time," Josh said.

"There *is* a significant amount of alien activity going on," Allen agreed. "I just wish I knew why."

The Journey of Allen Strange™

The Arrival

Invasion

Split Image

Legacy

Depth Charge

Alien Vacation (TV tie-in)

Election Connection

Available from MINSTREL Books

NICKELODEON®

the journey of

ALLEN STRANGE™

Election Connection

James Ponti

A MINSTREL® BOOK

Published by POCKET BOOKS
New York   London   Toronto   Sydney   Singapore

This book is a work of fiction. Names, characters, places and incidents are products of the author's imagination or are used fictitiously. Any resemblance to actual events or locales or persons living, or dead, is entirely coincidental.

A MINSTREL PAPERBACK *Original*

 A Minstrel Book published by
POCKET BOOKS, a division of Simon & Schuster Inc.
1230 Avenue of the Americas, New York, NY 10020

Copyright © 1999 by Viacom International Inc. All rights reserved. Based on the Nickelodeon series entitled *The Journey of Allen Strange*.

All rights reserved, including the right to reproduce this book or portions thereof in any form whatsoever. For information address Pocket Books, 1230 Avenue of the Americas, New York, NY 10020.

ISBN: 0-671-02514-7

First Minstrel Books printing November 1999

10 9 8 7 6 5 4 3 2

NICKELODEON, *The Journey of Allen Strange*, and all related titles, logos, and characters are trademarks of Viacom International Inc.

A MINSTREL BOOK and colophon are registered trademarks of Simon & Schuster Inc.

Front cover photo by Pat Hill Studio

Printed in the U.S.A.

For Terry and Cathy

CHAPTER
1

THURSDAY, 6:47 A.M.
PACIFIC POINT, NEAR DELPORT, CALIFORNIA

"*I* was shredding this unbelievably jacked wave when the lip up and axed me big-time," the teenager said as he shook some excess water from his shoulder-length hair. "It was total carnage!"

During his time on planet Earth, Allen Strange had studied the English language extensively, but he had absolutely no idea what this young man carrying a neon-blue surfboard was saying. Allen had been standing there observing when the boy came up

1

to him and started talking. Words like "axed" and "carnage" sounded bad, but the surfer was definitely happy. It just didn't make sense.

"Awesome," Robbie said, coming to Allen's rescue. "Just make sure you don't drop in on me when I catch that pipeline."

"No doubt," said the boy.

Now Allen had no idea what Robbie was saying, but it seemed to do the trick. The surfer smiled at them and rushed back out to the water with his board tucked under his arm.

"You understood him?" Allen asked.

"Sure," said Robbie. "He said he was riding a really big wave and then he crashed."

"Then why didn't he say *that!*" Allen asked. "He used some bizarre language, and you used it, too, when you talked to him."

"It's slang," she said with a shrug. "When in Rome, do as the Romans do."

"You mean he was speaking Italian?" Allen asked.

"No. That's a saying," explained Robbie. "It means you should adapt to the customs and language of the place you're visiting.

When you're on the beach, you've got to talk surfer dude."

"Very confusing," Allen said, shaking his head.

"You're the one who wanted to come down here with me," she said as she finished waxing her board.

"I want to learn," Allen answered. "I just don't know what to make of it." It was only a few minutes after sunrise and the beach was already flooded with surfers. "Is it always this crowded?"

"Not even," answered Robbie, strapping the tether line around her ankle. "Yesterday at this time, this beach was deserted."

"What happened?" Allen asked.

"That!" Robbie pointed to the ocean and a seemingly endless series of swells coming toward them. "Perfect waves for as far as the eye can see, and they're twice as high as usual."

Word had spread that Pacific Point was happening, and surfers had come from all over southern California—some had driven over one hundred miles—just to be there at daybreak.

3

"How did they know about the tidal change?" asked Allen. "Was it mentioned on the news or in the newspaper?"

Robbie shook her head. She had no real explanation. Your typical surfer might not be able to tell you much about current events, but he most definitely could tell you everything about currents in the ocean. "Surfers have a sixth sense about waves," she tried to explain. "They just *know* where to find them."

Robbie didn't *know* instinctively. She had overheard two guys talking about it at Zero's Surf Shop, where she worked after school. It was rare for her to surf this early in the morning, especially on a school day, but she couldn't wait until the weekend. By then the swells would probably have died down.

"Don't try to understand it all," Robbie said. "Just . . . *experience* it."

Allen nodded and Robbie smiled at him. Then she followed the others and ran out into the surf. Despite the crush of people, the beach was oddly quiet. This wasn't playtime. The crowd was taking the surfing seriously.

4

Robbie paddled out past the breakers, gently rising up and down with the swells. She didn't rush it and try to catch the first decent wave. She wanted to savor the whole atmosphere. As she lay on her board, she closed her eyes and took a deep breath.

Everything was perfect.

She wondered if Allen could ever understand why this moment was so right to her. He could figure out the physics of surfing and even appreciate the thrill of riding a wave. But she didn't know if he could feel the way she did about the smell of the salt air and the sound of the morning gulls flying overhead. She couldn't help but laugh at the thought of him trying to understand beach slang.

She always thought about Allen when she got on her surfboard. In an odd way, she felt closer to him when she was surfing than at any other time. She felt that way because she knew that the waves were caused by the moon's gravitational pull.

Her little surfboard was being powered by a giant rock in space over 250,000 miles away. When she thought about it that way,

5

she realized that she and Allen were all part of one . . . *something*. She didn't have a word for it, but it made her feel more connected to him.

She looked back over her shoulder and saw the wave—her wave. It was perfect. She didn't know why the waves were so high, but she didn't care. Her mother had been a champion surfer in high school and had told her once, "Never question the surf gods. Just enjoy the ride."

And that was what Robbie did.

She got up on her board and took off.

She almost wiped out in the first few seconds. The wave was much stronger than she'd expected. She bent down low and regained her balance. She went with the wave and waited for just the right moment to thrash, or cut back.

It was thrilling, an adrenaline rush like no other. A spray of water showered her face and the sound of the rushing wave was all she could hear. Now she really was like Allen—lost in another world rushing toward the beach—and she was having the time of her life.

"Never question the surf gods." She remembered her mother's words as her glorious ride came to an end. She looked over at another girl who had caught the same wave. They shared a smile.

"Liquid lightning," said the girl. The two of them paddled back out for another ride.

From his vantage point on the sand, Allen continued to watch his friend. He didn't quite understand why so many people had gotten up so early in the morning, but he tried to follow her advice and not overanalyze it. He tried to just *experience* what was happening around him.

Robbie was dying to describe her early morning surfing trip for her mother. She couldn't wait to call her mom and tell her all about it. Robbie didn't know why the waves had picked up, but she was too excited to worry about it. She was also too excited to notice the other change in the water.

In fact, most of the surfers were too excited to notice. But a few of the older guys did. The guys with the long boards and nicknames like Kona Bob. Those guys who lived to surf knew the ocean better than anybody

7

did, and they noticed a difference the moment they stepped into the surf. In addition to the waves getting bigger, something else was going on at Pacific Point.

For some unknown reason, the water was getting warmer.

CHAPTER 2

THURSDAY, 8:19 A.M.
DELPORT HIGH SCHOOL

"That was totally radical," Allen said trying out some of his new Surfspeak as they quickly sneaked down the hall. "Especially when you did that Wite-Out!"

Robbie stopped and tried to contain her laughter. "Wipeout," she said, correcting him. "Wite-Out is what you use to cover a mistake on paper."

"Right," Allen said making a mental note. "Wipeout."

They were trying to make it through the halls without getting caught. Robbie peeked

9

around the corner to make sure the coast was clear. "Unfortunately," added Robbie, "I wiped out one too many times. If I hadn't gone out for that one last wave, we wouldn't have been late for school."

But she had. And they were.

Convinced that no assistant principals were lurking behind the lockers, she led Allen down the next hall toward American history class. The tardy bell had rung four minutes earlier, but Robbie was hoping that their history teacher, Mr. Tyree, was still in the teachers' lounge getting his final jolt of wake-up coffee.

They reached the door to the classroom, which was decorated with a picture of Thomas Jefferson and a sign saying, All Men Are Created Equal. Students, Though, Are a Different Issue.

Robbie and Allen each took a breath and tried to slip into the room unnoticed. They made it two steps.

"Well, thank you for joining us, Ms. Stevenson and Mr. Strange," Mr. Tyree boomed from the front of the classroom. *So much for being unnoticed,* Robbie thought.

"Is there any reason why I shouldn't write you a tardy slip?" the teacher said, waving two blue pieces of paper in the air. He wasn't angry, but he wasn't going to let them get away with being late to class.

"Reason?" Allen said sheepishly.

Robbie tried to think quickly. A couple more tardy slips would mean detention and a letter home to her father. That would lead to a lecture and some sort of restriction. She wanted to beat this one. She looked desperately to Allen. Then she thought of something and blurted, "Delaware, sir."

Mr. Tyree gave her a quizzical look. "Delaware?"

Allen gave her an equally confused look.

She was going to go with this explanation. "Yes. Delaware. Last night we were doing our reading assignment on . . . " She started getting lost, so Allen came to her rescue.

"The Constitutional Convention," he said, jumping in. "We were studying together." He didn't know where this was going, but he was going to help if he could.

Mr. Tyree raised his eyebrows in anticipation. "And . . . ?"

11

"And . . . " Robbie was trying to make sure she remembered the facts correctly. "And we read about how the delegates from Delaware showed up late at the convention."

Allen was hoping she had more than this, but she didn't. She just looked at the teacher and smiled.

Mr. Tyree thought about this for a moment. "So you thought you'd demonstrate that point by arriving late yourself?" he offered.

"Right," Allen answered. "Just as though we were the delegates from Delaware."

Robbie completed the thought. "And this class were, in fact, the Continental Congress." Suddenly this was sounding like a good excuse. The two of them smiled. "Judging by our classmates' reactions, our demonstration obviously worked."

"Except," said the teacher, "that the delegation from Delaware wasn't late for the convention."

"It wasn't?" Robbie thought for sure she had it right.

"No," Mr. Tyree answered. "It was the delegation from Rhode Island."

So close, yet so far.

"Delaware . . . Rhode Island . . . I get all those little ones mixed up," Robbie said.

"Besides," Mr. Tyree continued. "Your hair's still wet and everybody knows the waves are kicking down at Pacific Point."

How does he know? Robbie asked herself. Mr. Tyree quickly filled out the tardy slips and held them out for the duo.

"I'm sure the surfing was worth the trouble," he whispered as Robbie took her slip from his hand.

"More than," Robbie agreed with a sly smile. She didn't really mind the tardy slip. She just kept thinking about that perfect wave. Besides, she couldn't get angry with Mr. Tyree. He was the most interesting teacher she had. He made history class fun.

Robbie and Allen took their seats. "Good try," he whispered.

History was Allen's favorite class. Unlike math and science, which were based on absolutes that ran throughout the universe, history was unique to each and every planet, place, and person. Because of this, history

13

was the class where Allen gained the most understanding about his new home.

Robbie and Allen had been right about the lesson. The class was studying the Constitutional Convention. But rather than lecture about it, Mr. Tyree had the students recreate it. He assigned different pairs of students to represent the various states. Then they all worked together to write their own constitution.

Playing off their failed excuse, the teacher made Robbie and Allen the delegates from Delaware. It was a fun class, and the two of them really got into it.

Allen pressed for, and won, an amendment for the formation of a government agency devoted to improving relations with distant planets and peoples. He finished his plea by saying, "What would happen if some alien arrived now? He'd probably wind up in somebody's attic." He winked at Robbie.

Robbie got into one particularly heated debate about the need to include the rights of women in the constitution. She was so convincing that the other delegates elected her president of the congress. She then failed in an attempt to give herself and Allen presidential pardons for being late.

After class, Mr. Tyree came over to Robbie and Allen as they gathered their books.

"Robbie," the teacher said.

"Yes, Mr. Tyree?" Robbie cringed. She was worried she was going to get a lecture about being late to class.

"About this morning," he continued, "when you came in late . . ."

"I am so sorry," she interjected. "It won't happen again. I just lost track of the time out there."

"No, not that," he said. "I was talking about your excuse. It was pretty good. I almost let you off the hook for creativity. And your speech about women's rights was excellent. Have you ever thought about running for student government?" he asked. "I'm the adviser, and elections are coming up."

"Yes!" Robbie said, a little more excited than she intended. "I mean, yes." This time she was less enthusiastic. "But I don't really think I'm the type."

"Really? I do. I think you'd be perfect," said Mr. Tyree. "You too, Allen. Although I don't think we need to have an intergalactic embassy here on campus."

Robbie and Allen exchanged knowing looks. *If only he knew how much one was needed,* Allen thought.

"It would be an honor," said Allen. "But I think I'm too new to the school to hold elective office. Robbie, though, would make a great candidate."

The teacher looked back at Robbie. He wasn't going to let her off the hook.

"Sure," Robbie said. "It would be great to be a class officer. But you have to give a speech, and I don't like talking in front of groups. Besides, school elections are nothing more than popularity contests. I don't think I'd get many votes."

"I'd vote for you," said Allen.

"Look at that. You haven't even started and you've already got a vote," Mr. Tyree said. "Who knows? If you tried, the election could turn into a landslide."

Robbie tried not to get swept up in the thought of running for office. "You know how it is, Mr. Tyree," she said. "The same kids always win."

"I know that's how it is," he said. "But I also know that it doesn't have to be that way."

THURSDAY, 12:40 P.M.
DELPORT HIGH SCHOOL CAFETERIA

Allen and Robbie were stuck in the middle of the cafeteria line waiting their turn to order. They stared at the options ahead of them, hoping that something—anything—might be edible.

"Amazing," said Robbie. "None of it even *looks* like food."

Allen had to agree. Even to an alien, the food looked pretty scary. He pointed to some sort of gravy or soup. "That has many of the same characteristics as pagma," he said, turning up his nose.

"What's pagma?" asked Robbie.

"It's a chemical secreted by Trykloids when they exert energy—"

"Allen" Robbie interrupted, "there's a decent chance I'm going to have to eat it, so please don't tell me it's alien sweat."

17

Allen nodded and stopped talking. Still, he was intrigued. He looked at the cafeteria lady as she scooped up food and put it on a tray.

"You know," he said. "Mrs. Thorson does have some Trykloidian traits. I wonder how many toes she has?"

"Can we please change the subject?" Robbie asked as she took her tray from the stack.

"Sure," said Allen. "Let's talk about student government. I think it's fascinating."

"What's fascinating about it?" Robbie asked.

"On Xela, we don't have a democracy like you do here," he explained. "We don't get to vote. Everything is decided by the Elders."

On Allen's home planet, the Elders were in the final stage of the life cycle. They had the wisdom of their own experience, and they had acquired the wisdom of past generations.

"I'm sure that's a much better system," Robbie answered. "The Elders are probably the smartest ones. They *should* make all of the decisions."

18

"Yes," said Allen. "But I really like the idea of democracy. The thought that each individual has some say in what is decided is very exciting."

"You like the idea of voting?" she asked.

"Absolutely," he answered.

"Good, it's your turn," said Robbie.

"What do you mean?" asked Allen.

She pointed to the food. "Mystery meat or alien sweat?"

Allen considered both. Neither seemed appealing. "You know," he answered, "I may go with 'none of the above' this time around."

Robbie thought about this. "Me too," she said.

The two of them put their trays back and slipped out of the line.

THURSDAY, 6:45 P.M.
THE STEVENSON HOUSE

"Mom, it was unbelievable," Robbie said excitedly into the phone. She was lying on her bed with her eyes closed, picturing the morning at the beach. "I've never seen waves that high. Each time I paddled out,

19

there was another wave slowly coming toward me, as if it had been—"

"Waiting for you," Gail Stevenson interjected.

"Exactly," Robbie answered. "As if it had been sent for me alone."

"I wish I could have seen it," her mother said. "What am I talking about? I wish I could have *surfed* it."

Ever since Gail Stevenson had moved to San Francisco to be a trauma nurse at a hospital, much of Robbie's relationship with her mother had been reduced to moments like this on the phone.

The relationship, like her parents' separation, was confusing and hard, but they both tried to make the most of it. Robbie loved those times when she and her mom got a chance to talk about something that was just theirs. Surfing was one of those things.

"I remember a day like that the summer before you were born," Gail continued. "I was up in Huntington Beach, and it was like an endless series of perfect waves."

Allen came into the room carrying a mountain of books. Robbie mouthed to him that she was talking to her mother. He was aware of how much Robbie valued any time with Gail. "You want me to leave?" he whispered. Robbie shook her head and Allen set his books down on the table.

"Was it crowded?" Robbie asked her mother about that day in Huntington Beach. "Or were you all alone?"

"Within a couple hours it looked like Times Square on New Year's Eve," she said with a laugh. "The whole world was there."

"How does everybody find out?" Robbie asked. "It's driving me crazy."

"Believe me," said Gail. "When there's something really good—*anything* really good—people have a way of learning about it."

Something about the hurried sound of her voice let Robbie know that her mother was running out of time. Gail hadn't said anything, but her daughter could always tell.

"Sounds like you've got to get going," Robbie offered.

Five hundred miles away, Gail cringed. She hated to rush off the phone, but she was due back on hospital rounds in a few

moments. "I'm sorry, honey," Gail answered. "I really do have to get back."

"I understand," said Robbie, although deep down she didn't really understand.

"I'll call you when my shift ends," Gail offered.

"I can't wait," said Robbie. "Talk to you then."

Robbie hung up the phone. She wished everything would suddenly get better with her parents. She wished her mother would move back home and the family would be together. But she knew that wasn't likely to happen. That she did understand.

Allen was deep in thought, speed-reading through all the books.

"Where were you after school?" Robbie asked.

"In the library," he answered. "I'm doing some research for a project."

"*Government in America, The Life of Theodore Roosevelt, Democracy in Action,*" she said, reading the titles of some of the books. "Did Mr. Tyree assign a report that I don't know about?"

"No," said Allen. "It's not a class project.

I got these books because I want to learn about your system of government. I think it's fascinating. Besides, that talk we had with Mr. Tyree got me thinking."

"About what?"

"Class elections," he answered. "I took your advice and got involved."

"Good for you," she said. "What are you doing?"

"I'm a campaign manager." Allen said it with great pride of achievement. "I want to read about campaigns of the past so I'll be better prepared to help my candidate win."

"That's great," said Robbie. "Who's the candidate?"

Allen smiled wide. "You are."

Robbie wasn't sure if she should laugh. But she sensed he wasn't joking. "That's impossible," she stuttered. "I'm not a candidate."

"Yes, you are," he said matter-of-factly. "I signed you up."

23

CHAPTER 3

"You did what?"

"I signed you up as a candidate." Allen was confused by Robbie's response. "Didn't you just hear me say that?"

"I heard it," Robbie replied. "I just can't believe it."

"I'm telling the truth," said Allen. "You can believe me." Allen still hadn't mastered the ability to understand whether people were being literal or using figures of speech.

Robbie was getting more and more exasperated. "How could you sign me up?"

"It was really quite simple. I only had to

24

write your name out on a nomination sheet and give it to Mr. Tyree. He was very excited, by the way." Allen gave up trying to understand Robbie's reaction and just smiled. "I think you'll do great."

"Well, you're wrong," she answered. "I won't do great, because there's no way I'm running."

"I don't understand," said Allen. "Didn't you say it would be great to be part of the student government?"

"Saying it'd be great is totally different from actually deciding to do it," Robbie explained. "I really don't think I can get elected, so it would be pointless to run. Besides, my dislike of public speaking makes giving a speech in front of the entire student body one of the worst experiences imaginable."

Robbie tried to think of a way out of the situation. Maybe she could just go to Mr. Tyree and quit the race. Maybe she could tell everyone it was just a joke. Maybe she could transfer to a different school.

"I still don't understand why you're upset," Allen said. "I think you'd make an excellent president."

25

"President?" wailed Robbie. "You nominated me for *president?*" The situation was getting worse by the second.

"Of course," said Allen. "You're overqualified for the other positions. By the way, what exactly does a sergeant at arms do? I didn't know the school had any military positions."

Robbie didn't answer. She was too busy thinking about her imminent doom. "You're still not getting it, Allen. Mike Archer is running for president," Robbie continued. "He's a basketball star. Everyone in school wants to be his friend. He's a lock to win."

"I don't know about that," Allen answered. "Some of the other kids think that Angie Gordon has a good chance of winning too." Allen was unaware that this would further upset Robbie.

"Angie Gordon is running?" Robbie couldn't believe it. "She's like the cutest cheerleader in school. I'm going to get creamed. Is there anyone else?"

"One more," said Allen. "Timmy Ryan."

For a brief moment, Robbie stopped worrying about her problems. Timmy Ryan was an even more unlikely candidate than she was. Awkward, skinny, and with a perpetual case of acne, Timmy had been picked on since he moved to Delport five years ago. Robbie really liked him and felt protective of him. She couldn't imagine him doing well in a school campaign. Then again, she couldn't imagine herself doing well, either.

Robbie tried to calm herself by taking deep breaths. "Maybe I'll come in third."

"That's the spirit," Allen said, still not quite getting it.

THURSDAY, 7:56 P.M.
CABLE 3 TELEVISION STUDIO

It was four minutes to airtime and Phil Berg was getting very excited about the upcoming episode of *Watch the Skies*. The series was dedicated to proving the existence of alien beings and their presence on Earth, and Berg thought that this episode was about to take it, in his words, "to another level."

He had a nervous bounce as he walked

27

across the chilly studio to his chair. He kept the temperature cold so that he wouldn't sweat during the show. He wanted to look cool and confident. "Tonight will be one for the history books," he said to one of the camera operators.

Although he wasn't running for office, Berg found himself in his own race for votes. He was in a popularity contest with other shows—shows that were better known and better looking. He was competing for votes that came in the form of ratings. If the ratings of *Watch the Skies* didn't improve, the show would soon find itself banished to the 3 A.M. time slot right after *Bingorama*.

With that in mind, Phil had pulled out all the stops for this episode. He had gone so far as to call it a *Watch the Skies* special report. He had even sent press releases to local newspapers about the show and its new revelation, the Monument Beacons theory.

This particular revelation had occurred to Berg the previous week when he came across a dusty old globe that had long been locked in one of Cable 3's storage closets. That same globe was now polished and sitting on a podium amid large-scale models of the Eiffel Tower and the Leaning Tower of Pisa. That globe might be the turning point in his career.

"Good evening and welcome to a *Watch the Skies* special report," Berg said as he opened the show. "Tonight I will show you evidence that proves beings from other planets have been using our Earth as a meeting place for thousands of years. Tonight I will uncover the truth about . . . the Monument Beacons."

There was a gleam in Berg's eye. He was cool and confident. This revelation was going to knock his viewers' socks off.

THURSDAY, 8:12 P.M.
THE STEVENSON HOUSE

With at least one viewer, Berg was right on track. Josh Stevenson, Robbie's younger brother, was mesmerized as the television host explained his Monument Beacons theory.

Berg explained that "A straight line can be

29

drawn that connects Stonehenge in England to the Eiffel Tower in Paris, Italy's Leaning Tower of Pisa, and the Great Pyramid of Cheops in Egypt."

He demonstrated this on the globe he had found in the storage closet. He added that it was "a statistical impossibility that four of the most famous objects in history would be built in a straight line merely by coincidence."

Then he dropped his bombshell. "I contend that these supposedly man-made structures are actually beacons that point to an alien landing surface that is now submerged beneath the surface of the Indian Ocean. The monuments are just like the runway lights you see at airports."

Josh was loving it. Like Berg, he was convinced that the arrangement of these buildings couldn't be coincidental. This was earth-shattering. He excitedly called upstairs. "Robbie! Allen! You gotta come watch this."

Then the host dropped another bombshell.

"It is quite likely," Berg said, drawing out

his words for dramatic effect, "that this underwater landing strip is in fact the lost continent of Atlantis." Another dramatic pause. "More on that in a moment."

The show cut to a commercial, and Josh bolted upstairs to find Robbie and Allen. "You guys have got to come see the *WTS* special report," he said as he burst through the door.

"*WTS?*" asked Robbie.

"*Watch the Skies*," Josh replied. In the Internet chat rooms Josh frequented, fans had taken to calling it *WTS* to save time typing.

"I don't have time for *WTS*," she answered. "I'm too busy with SOS."

"SOS?" Now Josh was confused.

"Save old Stevenson," Robbie answered. She gave Allen a pointed look.

"Apparently I confused Robbie's theoretical interest in running for class president with her practical knowledge that it was highly unlikely she would win," Allen explained.

"You're running for class president?" Josh was amazed. He knew his sister was afraid

31

to speak in public. "And you say *I'm* crazy."

"See what I mean?" Robbie asked Allen. "I'm going to lose."

"You better hope you do," said Josh. "You better hope you come in dead last."

"Why would she want to do poorly?" asked Allen.

"Well, for one thing, counterintelligence," he said. "Especially if you propose any big ideas. They'll want you out of the race before the actual election day. You don't want to battle the CIA."

Robbie rolled her eyes. "Don't start that again."

"What?" Josh asked defiantly. "Don't start telling the truth?"

"There is not a conspiracy organization rigging high school class elections," an exasperated Robbie countered. "I think the government has more important things to do than worry about student council."

"You're so naive," Josh answered. "The same people who covered up the alien invasion at Roswell work on everything from the Congress down to student government." He turned to Allen and explained,

"They practice their methods on impressionable young minds to see how the techniques work."

"No, they don't," Robbie said.

"Okay," Josh offered. "Ask yourself this. Do the same kids always win these elections?"

"Maybe," Robbie answered. "So?"

"Why do they win?" Josh was using dramatic pauses, trying to lay out his idea just as Berg had laid out his new theory. "Do you think the winners have the best ideas?"

"Of course not," said Robbie.

"Do you think they are more capable of leading the class?" Josh continued.

"Get to the point," said Robbie.

"Why do they get elected?" He said this as if making some great pronouncement: "Because of the conspiracy."

Robbie and Allen gave him blank looks.

"Anyway," Josh continued. "*Watch the Skies* is way cool tonight. You've got to come see it."

He could tell they were uninterested, so he dismissed them with a wave of his hand and rushed back downstairs.

33

8:17 P.M. PACIFIC STANDARD TIME
13,000 MILES FROM EARTH

An incredibly dense compound of ice and salt blazed a path directly toward Earth. No bigger than a golf ball, the compound was not the exciting stuff of Martian invasions, or even the Monument Beacons theory that Phil Berg was broadcasting at that precise moment.

Space debris like this blob regularly made contact with the Earth. Typically, this debris burned up upon reaching the planet's protective atmosphere. But the space junk that did make it to the surface offered information to scientists who studied the cosmos. This one was much too small, though. Pieces this size never survived all the way to the surface.

Well, almost never.

For some reason this piece of junk did survive. As it reached the edge of the atmosphere, a thin blue layer of energy enveloped it and protected it from the extreme heat. A burst of flames shot from it like the tail of a comet, but nothing melted the ice or the salt. To a scientist, this development would have been far more exciting than whether or not the Eiffel Tower helped point to a secret alien landing strip.

Certainly any NASA specialist would have loved to study the rock to find out why it didn't burn up. But there was no chance of that happening. The rock landed deep in the middle of Carbon Canyon and continued down into the ground. Nobody would find it. This space invader was perfectly anonymous.

THURSDAY, 8:26 P.M.
THE STEVENSON HOUSE

Despite all her protests, Robbie was actually excited that she was running for class president. It was the type of thing that she always considered but never did. She would never have entered the race on her own, but Allen had taken care of that for her. She was running. She might as well do her best.

"Okay, Mr. Campaign Manager," Robbie said to Allen. "What do we do first?"

Allen had used his powers to speed-read the U.S. Constitution and the history books he'd gotten at the library. They gave him an unrealistically idealized vision of democracy.

35

"First we need to start shaping your platform," he said. "Your views on the key issues, such as health care reform, Social Security, and poverty."

"It's *class* president," said Robbie. "I don't think I have much say in health care reform."

"You also need to decide on your running mate," he said. "A vice presidential candidate who'll fill out your ticket. Many presidents pick running mates who live in large states like Texas or California. That way they attract a lot of extra voters."

"Everyone at school lives in Delport," Robbie said.

"Good point," said Allen. "Maybe you should get someone from a big homeroom."

She laughed. "I was kidding, Allen. High school candidates don't usually have running mates."

Robbie didn't want to admit it to herself, but she was getting excited about the election. She had always wondered what it would be like to be one of the kids in the spotlight: extra pictures in the yearbook, invitations to all the parties.

"Unbelievable," Josh said as he entered the attic. "There is no way for the government to cover up the Monument Beacons theory. This is very big."

"What are you talking about?" asked Robbie.

"Phil Berg's new theory," said Josh. "It's amazing. It's all about how Earth is nothing more than a big intergalactic airport."

In the distance, dogs started to bark. Then they heard a strange noise: *whoop, whoop whoop*. It was some type of alarm. Before they could figure it out, another one started up: *honk, honk, honk*.

Then another. Soon they were nearly deafened by the sound of car alarms going off. The three of them rushed to the window.

"Berg was right," Josh shouted excitedly. "Here they come!"

The alarms got closer and closer, louder and louder. But it wasn't a sign of some alien invasion. It was worse.

Then the walls of the house started to shake!

37

CHAPTER 4

8:31 P.M.
THE STEVENSON HOUSE

"What's happening?" Allen asked, as the house that had always seemed rock-solid suddenly started to jiggle like a bowl of Jell-O.

"Earthquake!" Robbie and Josh shouted in unison.

"Quick!" said Robbie. "Get to the doorway!"

Ken Stevenson had taught his kids exactly what to do in case of a tremor. They hurried over to the doorway, which was structurally the strongest part of the room. Allen,

38

though, didn't follow them. He seemed stuck in the middle of the room, his face shaking back and forth.

"Allen!" Robbie called. "Come over here!"

"I-I-I can't-t-t-t-t!" he said, his words skipping like a compact disc that is stuck. The power of the earthquake traveled through him, and Allen's features started blurring and warping. For an instant his body stretched like Silly Putty. Then it exploded into countless balls of blue energy.

The balls bounced around the room and provided a dizzying array of blue and silver blurs. Robbie and Josh had no idea what they should do.

8:32 P.M.
CABLE 3 TELEVISION STUDIO

"Get us back on the air!" Phil Berg shouted into his microphone. He couldn't believe it. *Watch the Skies* had ended and Phil had gone to a commercial break just moments before the tremors started. This was exactly the kind of moment he wanted to report on live television. He certainly wasn't going to miss it by a few minutes.

39

"Get us back on the air, I said!" he roared into his microphone.

In the control booth, the show's director, Alison Liddi, sat at a console full of television monitors, buttons, and levers. There was one monitor for each of the cameras on the studio floor and another that showed what was being broadcast. At that moment the broadcast monitor was showing a commercial for Fizzies candy.

A blue turtle was dancing on the screen and singing, "So what is he? He's a Fizzie!"

Alison pressed a button that let her speak to Phil by way of an earpiece that was unseen by the home audience. "I can't interrupt a commercial," she said. "The sponsors pay the bills."

Another tremor shook the *Watch the Skies* set. The model of the Leaning Tower of Pisa leaned even more. Berg was getting impatient. He wanted the tower to fall over. But he wanted it to topple while he was on the air. That would be really dramatic. He also wanted to beat the competition.

He knew it would take ten or fifteen minutes for the other stations to get their news crews on television. He could beat them all and break this story. He could shape what everyone else thought for a change. First he had exposed the Monument Beacons theory; now he was going to broadcast an earthquake live.

"Just do it," he barked.

Liddi waited until the very end of the commercial: "'Cause everyone knows Fizzies are fun!" Then she quickly pulled a lever. The commercial faded away and was replaced by the *Watch the Skies* logo.

Phil turned to camera one. He took a deep breath and waited for the red light above the lens to come on. When he saw it, he started.

"Ladies and gentlemen, we interrupt our scheduled programming to bring you a breaking story. Southern California is being hit by a series of earthquakes."

Another shock wave rattled the studio, and Phil looked up at the giant lights shaking in the rigging. He quickly checked to make sure there were none directly above him. Then he continued.

"Earthquakes are common throughout

41

this area. Perhaps they are too common. It is the opinion of this reporter that the high frequency of earthquakes has lulled us into acceptance. Most of us don't question our government officials when they tell us the epicenter or origin of these quakes. But *I* do question them.

"Many educated people feel that some earthquakes are actually the result of underground government testing and of alien arrivals. Under cover of these so-called natural disasters, the government is able to keep these tests and landings from public scrutiny. Only time will tell whether this quake is the result of the shifting of continental plates beneath the surface of the earth, or if it is in fact the result of something far more sinister. One thing I can promise: this reporter won't rest until the truth is known."

Another tremor hit. It wasn't huge, but it was big enough to knock over the Leaning Tower model. First the Monument Beacons theory and now this. Phil Berg could barely contain his excitement. This was his night of nights. He was certain he was about to become a star.

THURSDAY, 8:33 P.M.
THE STEVENSON HOUSE

Robbie's heart was racing. As if the earthquake wasn't bad enough, Allen was still bouncing around the attic in the form of a thousand blue energy balls. Josh watched in amazement, trying in vain to track the balls as they ricocheted off of the still trembling walls.

The tremor finally ended, and the house settled back down. After a few moments the balls started to glob together and rebuild Allen from the feet up. It took about ten seconds, so for a brief period, Josh and Robbie saw just his legs, then his arms, and finally his entire body. He still looked a little blurry, but then there was one final snap and he looked like the Allen of old.

"Radical," Allen said, borrowing some of the lingo he had picked up at the beach that morning. "Talk about your wipeouts."

Robbie and Josh sighed once they realized

43

that Allen had actually enjoyed his little experience. "So you're all right?" asked Josh.

"Perfect," said Allen. "That was wonderful. The entire world moved."

"I wouldn't call it wonderful," said Robbie. "Earthquakes make me . . . shaky."

"I've only studied them until now," said Allen, "but the experience is exhilarating. We don't have earthquakes on Xela; the seas of energy absorb any movement. I guess that's what my energy was trying to do."

Just then one remaining blue energy ball whipped past Allen. "Oops, I must have missed that one." The ball rebounded off of the bedpost, bounced off the ceiling, and caromed up from the floor. Allen reached out and caught it in his palm just as Ken Stevenson walked into the room.

"Is everyone okay?" Ken said.

"We're fine, Dad," answered Robbie. "No damage in here." Allen still had the energy ball in his hand and it was glowing. He didn't want Ken to see it, so Allen put it in his mouth like a piece of candy.

44

"How about you?" Ken said to Allen.

Allen couldn't answer without the ball shooting out of his mouth, so he just nodded.

"He's fine," said Robbie, coming to his rescue. "He's just a little spooked."

"That's understandable," said Ken. "Was that your first earthquake?"

Allen swallowed the energy ball with a gulp. "Yes."

Right then Ken's pager went off. He unhooked it from his belt and checked the readout, even though he was pretty certain what it was. "DIRT," he said.

Robbie and Josh knew exactly what he was talking about, but Allen was confused. "Dirt?" he asked. "You mean like soil?"

"No, D.I.R.T.," said Ken. "Delport Instant Response Team. I've got to get down to the office." As a city planner, Ken Stevenson was part of the team that quickly assembled in case of any public emergency. An earthquake with a Richter scale reading over 4.0 automatically required DIRT members to report.

"Do you guys want to come with me, or

45

would you rather stay here?" Ken asked, looking at his kids.

"Stay!" Robbie and Josh blurted out. Experience taught them that going with their father on a DIRT mission meant sitting around the basement of City Hall all night. It was beyond dull.

"Okay," said Ken. "But I want you to stay downstairs and in the front of the house for a while in case there are any aftershocks."

Ken quickly scanned the room for damage. Then something caught his eye. It was a poster on the table in front of Allen and it read, Vote for Stevenson!

"What's that?" Ken asked.

"Campaign materials," said Allen.

"I'm kind of running for class president," said Robbie, still not used to the idea.

This caught Ken by surprise. "That's great," he said. "But are you sure you have enough time? I don't want it to cut into your studies."

"Don't worry, Dad," she said. "It's not like I'll win or anything."

"Don't sell yourself short," he said. "Anyway, Allen, I'm sure your parents are worried about you. You better get home."

"Yes, Mr. Stevenson," he said. "You're probably right."

"See you tomorrow Allen," said Robbie.

Allen smiled and said his good-byes. Then he exited out the front door, only to levitate back up to the attic window. He watched from above as Ken gave both kids a hug and a kiss. There was something different about it, Allen noticed. The hugs lasted just a moment longer than usual.

THURSDAY, 11:35 P.M.
CABLE 3 TELEVISION STUDIO

Phil Berg sat back in his chair and watched his competitors. He used the remote control to surf the channels on the big screen television in his boss's office. Normally, Phil wasn't allowed in here, but it was late and no one else was around. Berg wanted to see if anyone had picked up on his lead.

He had stopped broadcasting over two and a half hours ago. At that point he really couldn't compete with the bigger stations. Their news departments had crews span-

47

ning the area, looking for damage from the earthquake.

He flipped to channel 5 and saw a seismologist talking about the quake. It was officially registered as a 4.7 on the Richter scale and its epicenter was in Carbon Canyon.

"Carbon Canyon" Phil said out loud. He grabbed a notepad and wrote, "4.7—Carbon Canyon."

Then he switched to channel 8's E-Team coverage. Phil wasn't sure if the *E* stood for "emergency" or "earthquake," but he had to admit that it was a catchy name.

There was little damage around Delport, which meant there wasn't much to show on television. To counter that, the reporters had to talk more, which left them scrambling for different angles.

It led one of the E-Team reporters to mention Phil Berg's theory. Britney Soward was reporting while standing in front of a broken fire hydrant. As the water sprayed into the air, Soward said, "There have even been some reports of people believing the earthquake was the result of a secret government test."

"There it is," Berg shouted gleefully. "I got the word out." Berg didn't even let it bother him that Soward had left off the part about alien landings. He was thrilled that he had helped start the story. He was beginning to have an impact on the community.

He looked back down at the notepad. "Carbon Canyon." Maybe there was a story there. Berg began thinking about his next step. He kicked back and kept watching in case someone else picked up on the story.

FRIDAY, 6:45 A.M.
PACIFIC POINT

Although Robbie didn't return for another early morning ride, the beach was once again jammed with surfers at sunrise. The waves at Pacific Point were monstrous, just as they had been a day earlier. And just as they had done a day earlier, surfers had come from all over, searching for the perfect ride on the perfect wave.

There were all types of surfers, old and young, male and female. They represented every aspect of beach culture. But two of them were different from the others.

49

Ed and Fred hardly looked out of place. Ed was tall and lanky and had stringy blond hair. Fred was shorter and dark and had a shaved head. They both wore dark wraparound sunglasses, which wasn't unusual. What was odd about the pair was that beneath those sunglasses each had six eyes. And while some of the other surfers had come from as far away as four hundred miles, Ed and Fred had traveled 3.7 light-years.

CHAPTER
5

FRIDAY, 8:02 A.M.
DELPORT HIGH SCHOOL

Robbie hadn't even considered going back to Pacific Point the next morning. Except for the earthquake, she hadn't been able to think about anything but the election since Allen first told her about it.

She wanted to get a feel for the idea that she was running for class president. She wanted to walk around the school before classes started, as if she'd be able to sense whether or not she had any chance of winning.

51

By the time she reached the library, her chances seemed less than slim. Mike Archer had flooded the school with campaign materials. Everywhere she looked, she saw students wearing red, white, and blue buttons proclaiming, "I Like Mike."

He even had campaign posters on what seemed to be half the walls in the building. Robbie stopped to look at one. It had Mike's face pasted onto a picture of Robin Hood shooting a bow and arrow, and it read, Hit the Bull's-eye with Archer! Robbie thought it was corny but kind of funny. She couldn't help but think, *It's the first day of the election campaign and Mike has already won.*

"Unbelievable, isn't it?" said a voice. Robbie turned to see the perpetually perky smile of fellow candidate Angie Gordon. "It's like he wallpapered the school."

"They're everywhere," Robbie responded. She was surprised. She barely knew Angie and couldn't remember the last time they had talked to each other.

"Anyway," Angie continued. "I just wanted to wish you the best of luck in the campaign. I really, really want to win. But if it isn't me, I hope it's you."

"Right," said Robbie. She wondered how Angie even knew she was running. "Me too. I mean, if it isn't me, I hope it's you."

"I better get back on the campaign trail," the cheerleader said with a wink. "I'll see you later." With that, Angie disappeared into a group of kids over by the lockers.

That was weird, Robbie thought.

Just then her friend Erika Larson came rushing up the hall. "Robbie! I can't believe you didn't tell me about this."

"What?" asked Robbie, who was still trying to figure out why Angie Gordon had come over to talk to her.

"The *election,*" Erika interjected. "I mean, I'm only your best friend."

"Right, the election." Robbie realized she should have called Erika and mentioned it. "It was kind of a sudden thing, yesterday."

"Well, I think it's great. But there's not a lot of time." Erika started rattling off a list. "We're going to have to work on campaign strategy. We'll need signs, buttons, and of

course a banner for the cafeteria. And get this: T-shirts."

Robbie wasn't exactly sure why Erika was so gung-ho about the election. "That sounds great," Robbie said. "But won't that cost a lot of money?"

"We'll have to do it on the cheap," Erika said. "But isn't that what campaign managers are supposed to take care of?"

Erika was smiling, but Robbie wasn't. Allen was already her campaign manager. After all, it had been his idea for her to run in the first place. But Robbie knew it would hurt Erika's feelings if she thought Robbie was picking Allen over her. She didn't know what to say, so she just smiled and hoped a solution would come to her.

8:15 A.M.

"Lookee here," Mr. Tyree said, walking into the room as the bell rang. "The delegation from Delaware has decided to show up on time today." This brought a chorus of laughs from the class. Robbie and Allen flashed smiles.

"And for those who don't know," the teacher continued, "our Ms. Stevenson has decided to run for class president."

Robbie half expected the others to laugh, but instead, the response was favorable. Most of the people smiled. One even shouted a rousing "All right, Robbie!" Suddenly Robbie began to think that running for president might not be so bad after all.

FRIDAY, 12:15 P.M.
CARBON CANYON

A sweat-stained Phil Berg tromped down into Carbon Canyon. The television host wasn't sure exactly what he was looking for, just something—anything—that might help his show.

He lugged an array of equipment—a camcorder, a shovel, even a Geiger counter to measure radioactivity. Berg's goal was to find something he could showcase that night on *Watch the Skies*. He had been the first to suggest that something sinister might have caused the earthquake. Now he was going into its epicenter to search for evidence.

55

12:42 P.M.
DELPORT HIGH SCHOOL CAFETERIA

Robbie and Allen were sitting on the patio digging into their bag lunches. The lunches were a response to the poor cafeteria selection the day before. Robbie had opted to make peanut butter and jelly sandwiches rather than run the risk of eating alien sweat. The patio was an attempt to be seen. She was running for president and had to be seen by everybody. Angie Gordon and Mike Archer ate outside. Even Timmy Ryan did. In subtle ways, the election was already having an affect on her.

"We've really got to work on your campaign speech," Allen said, taking a bite of his sandwich. "You keep putting it off."

"I don't want to think about speaking in public," Robbie replied with a smile. "You see, when I think about it, I start to visualize everybody in the world sitting there looking at me. Then I get all queasy. Then I start to think about how I got in this mess and who I can blame." She gave him a look with raised eyebrows.

"You mean me?" Allen asked.

"Yes, I mean you," said Robbie. "You're the one who got me into this."

"It wasn't my idea to have speeches," he said with a laugh. "I'm just your campaign manager."

"Her what?" The voice came from behind Allen and Robbie. They turned to see a surprised Erika.

"I'm Robbie's campaign manager," Allen said, not understanding.

Erika tried to hide her hurt feelings. "I thought you said *I* was your campaign manager," she stated to Robbie.

"Actually," Robbie answered, "you *assumed* you were my campaign manager. I just didn't correct you. I was worried you'd think I was picking Allen over you."

"Which you are," Erika replied. "Aren't you?"

"No," said Robbie. "It wasn't really a choice. Allen signed me up for the election. It was his idea for me to run in the first place."

"It's too bad you didn't feel that you could

57

tell me that," said Erika. "I guess you think I'm too sensitive or something."

Robbie realized that she should have set the record straight in the first place. Now Erika's feelings were hurt. She tried to make it better. "I know," Robbie offered. "You and Allen could be co–campaign managers."

"Thanks, but no thanks," Erika said. "I don't need you to be involved in things. I can do just fine."

"Erika?" The voice was from the next bench. It belonged to Timmy Ryan. "If you really want to work on a campaign, I'm kind of looking for a campaign manager."

Erika thought about it for a second. "Great," she said. "You've just found one."

Timmy smiled and the two shook hands.

3:20 P.M.
CARBON CANYON

Just when he was about to give up on his expedition, Phil Berg took one last pass with his Geiger counter and came across something. Berg's eyes opened wide as the meter began to register slightly elevated amounts of radioactivity. He didn't know what had caused that elevation, but it didn't matter. He had accused the government of cover-ups concerning earthquakes and here was something suspicious at the epicenter of an earthquake.

Berg decided instantly that he would do another *Watch the Skies* special report: "The Phantom Tremors." The only thing missing was a good visual to go with his story. For his Monument Beacons show, he had used models of the Eiffel Tower and the Leaning Tower of Pisa, but those had been built for a European-cooking show that also ran on Cable 3.

He'd need some kind of model for this special report as well. But he didn't have the time, or the skill, necessary to make such a model. Then he had a brainstorm.

"Why build a model," he said aloud, "when I can do the show live from here?" He looked around at his surroundings. It was only scrub and sand. But in his mind he saw television lights, cameras, and—best of all—a mob of adoring fans.

4:30 P.M.
THE STEVENSON HOUSE

"She's not going to answer," Allen said.

A frustrated Robbie let the phone ring a couple more times before slapping it back into the cradle. She had called Erika every fifteen minutes since getting home from school, but her best friend hadn't answered. "She has Caller I.D.," she said by way of explanation. "She knows it's me."

"Maybe she's not home," offered Allen. "She could be with Timmy Ryan somewhere, working on their campaign."

Robbie couldn't believe she had let this happen. Not only had she managed to hurt Erika's feelings, but now Erika was running a rival campaign.

"I'm sure you'll be able to make this up to her," said Allen. "But it's going to take a little time."

"You're probably right," said Robbie. "I'm just upset with myself. And I'm a little worried about how the election will go for them."

"Well, you'd better start worrying about

how it will go for you," said Allen. "Everyone else has started campaigning. We need to get the word out about you."

"I've got an idea," said Josh, who had wandered in from the family room.

"What is it?" asked Alan.

"I was thinking you could be like those people on the *Today* show," said Josh. "You know, the ones who stand outside the studio window and hold up signs. It's a free way to get on television. And everyone knows that elections are won by television advertising."

"Interesting," said Allen.

"Except for one thing," offered Robbie. "The *Today* show is in New York and we're in Delport."

"Good point," agreed Allen.

"Thank you, Ms. Map!" exclaimed Josh. "I was thinking more of a local show. I just read in the *Watch the Skies* chat room that Phil Berg is taping on location tonight in Carbon Canyon."

"Why there?" asked Robbie. "What's in Carbon Canyon?"

"It has something to do with the earthquake," answered Josh. "If it's anything like his Monument Beacons theory, it will be amazing."

6:00 P.M.
PACIFIC POINT

A large black van pulled into the parking lot overlooking the beach. It looked like any other dark van with tinted windows. The only hint of what went on inside the van was its license plate: ARC 4.

ARC was the acronym for the Alien Retrieval Commission, a multinational organization formed to protect the planet from alien invaders. This dark van was ARC's latest weapon in its war with extraterrestrials. It contained state-of-the-art tracking devices and was hooked up to a communications grid with the military and intelligence communities. Like everyone else, ARC had come to Pacific Point to check out the big waves. Unlike the fun-loving surfers, however, it had come specifically to question the surf gods and find out the reason behind the enormous waves.

7:48 P.M.
CARBON CANYON

Like the men from ARC, Phil Berg was looking for answers. And he expected to find them—and an audience—in Carbon Canyon. He wasn't actually broadcasting from the spot where he'd registered the readings on the Geiger counter. Instead, he was at a nearby picnic ground that had the electrical outlets necessary for the cameras and lights. But he was close enough for the dramatic effect he was after.

Robbie, Allen, and Josh were among the crowd of about thirty people who had come down to see Berg tape his show. Josh had persuaded the others to come, but not because of his campaigning idea. He'd told them about Berg's Monument Beacons theory, and they had to admit that it was intriguing. Maybe he was onto something. Although most of the world thought Berg was a crackpot, they realized that he sometimes came close to uncovering true signs of alien existence. And they were always on the lookout for any way Allen could get in touch with his home planet.

63

Berg would have liked more people in the crowd, but there hadn't been much time to spread the word. Besides, the area would look packed on television, and that was what mattered. Most of the people had come because of the giant searchlight Berg had borrowed from the car dealership where his cousin worked.

"Check it out," said Josh, pointing toward some people over by the searchlight. "I think they're a little lost."

Robbie and Allen looked over at the people Josh was pointing at. Two surfers, still in their bathing suits and bare feet, were poking the ground with a stick.

"Just a bit," said Robbie.

"Maybe I'll try my surfing lingo with them," said Allen. "I've been practicing all day."

Before they could stop him, Allen started over to the duo. Robbie and Josh were right behind him.

"Hello," said Allen. "Were you hanging ten down at the beach today?"

The surfer called Ed didn't answer the

question. He just said, "Dude," as though they were old buddies.

"Shredding," said Fred, equally enthusiastic.

Robbie and Josh exchanged curious looks.

"You guys surf?" asked Robbie.

"Wipeout jacked waves hang ten," said Fred.

"Rip, curl, saturate," said Ed. The two smiled and walked off.

Robbie couldn't make any sense of what they said. "Now I know how you feel," Robbie said to Allen. "I thought I spoke surfer-dude well, but I didn't understand a thing they said."

"That's because they aren't surfers," explained Allen.

"What do you mean?" Josh said.

"They're aliens," replied Allen. "My guess is Celuvians."

Josh looked back over at Ed and Fred, who were once again probing the ground with a stick. "Surfer aliens?"

"Celuvians are scouts," Allen said. "They go on expeditions to check out an area. They

65

replicate the first dominant life form they encounter."

"Which means they must have made first contact at the beach," Robbie said.

"Right," said Allen. "They just don't realize that's not how everyone dresses. And it will take them at least a couple kerbots to figure out the language. They're not too smart."

As they talked, they watched Ed and Fred, who were still looking around. Allen couldn't figure out why they were there. Unlike Robbie and Josh, however, he didn't find their presence strange. Humans still had problems accepting that there were other life-forms in the universe, but Allen was used to the concept.

"They're obviously looking for something," Josh concluded.

"Yeah," said Robbie. "I wonder what it could be."

"Depends on their mission," said Allen. "They could be looking for anything from food to new energy sources. They're harmless. It's not like they're Trykloids or anything."

Just then Phil Berg's stage manager shouted to everybody. "Ladies and gentlemen, we're about to start taping the show, so if you'll please come over here." He motioned them to an area next to the camera. A stage had been set up in the parking lot overlooking the canyon.

Phil started talking to the crowd as they all got together. "I want to thank you all for coming down here tonight. This is going to be a very important show, and I think you'll all be glad you're seeing it firsthand. Be prepared for a question-and-answer session where I'll talk to some of you on camera."

Josh got excited. *Watch the Skies* was his favorite show. He'd have loved to be on it debating alien theories with Phil Berg. He quickly tried to come up with a couple of good questions to ask the host. He even thought about using the Celuvians somehow.

Phil took his place on a director's chair and looked at the camera. He waited for the red light to signal he was on the air. When it blinked, he started.

67

"Welcome to a *Watch the Skies* special report. Today I am talking to you from Carbon Canyon, the epicenter of yesterday's earthquake. Interestingly, this epicenter is located in a fault line that was previously unknown. At least that's the explanation our government has given us."

Berg held up his Geiger counter for dramatic effect. "But earlier today this Geiger counter discovered an inexplicable amount of radiation in the canyon. I'd like to hear how our government explains that."

He looked straight at the camera, and then, just as he went to make another bold statement, the red light flickered off. In an instant everything—the television equipment, the searchlight, anything that used electricity—went dead. As Phil and the crowd tried to figure out what was happening, all of Delport was plunged into darkness.

CHAPTER
6

**FRIDAY, 8:04 P.M.
CARBON CANYON**

"Cover-up!" Berg shouted into his suddenly darkened surroundings. "This is a government cover-up!" He was certain that some secret agency had pulled the plug on his electricity because he was too close to revealing the truth. He was on to something and *they* didn't want the world to find out about it. He had to find a way to get his message out to the people. Then he spied the electrical generator at the back of the production truck.

"Quick," he yelled to his director. "Crank up that generator! We can still broadcast!"

69

"It's pointless," she responded. "The whole town is out of power. Even if we could broadcast, no one would be able to watch us." Under her breath she added, "Not that it would be much different than usual."

Allen and Robbie looked around. The director was right. The blackout stretched for as far as they could see. The only sources of light were the nearly full moon and the dimming glow of the searchlight, which took a few moments to fade out completely.

Berg was ranting. "First the earthquake! Now the blackout! Something is definitely going on!" He stalked off the set and climbed into the back of the production truck. There was a police scanner in there, and he wanted to hear what was going on.

"Talk about paranoid," Robbie commented once he had passed them. "You know, sometimes earthquakes and power outages just happen."

"Hey," said Josh. "What happened to those surfer aliens? They've disappeared."

Robbie and Allen looked around. There

was enough moonlight to see everyone in the crowd, and the Celuvians were definitely gone. Allen had been keeping an eye on them, but he had been momentarily distracted by the blackout.

Allen was perplexed. "Celuvians can't become invisible," he said, "but they can move very fast. They must have slipped away when I wasn't paying attention."

"Maybe they caused the blackout," said Josh. "They could have been worried that Berg was going to uncover them on the air."

"Doubtful," said Allen. "Like I said, Celuvians are not too bright. I don't think they'd be able to do this much damage by themselves. If they wanted to stop Phil Berg they would just ionize him."

Robbie and Josh shared a look. They weren't sure what being ionized entailed, but it didn't sound good.

"So what do you guys want to do?" asked Allen. "Wait around here?"

"Nah," said Robbie. "I don't think much is going to happen here." To Phil Berg's dismay, the crew was already preparing to dismantle the set.

"I'll tell you what I'd like to do," said Josh. "I want to find out what caused this blackout."

"How would you do that?" asked Allen.

Robbie thought of something. "I think I know how—DIRT."

8:27 P.M.
CITY HALL

It took the trio twenty minutes to ride their bikes from Carbon Canyon to City Hall. As they went, Allen was amazed at how dependent humans were on electricity. Traffic lights had stopped, backing up cars everywhere. Stores and restaurants were closed. Few people seemed to be prepared for such an occurrence.

City Hall itself was being powered by an emergency generator, which only worked a few strategically placed backup lights. The lights gave the hallways a spooky kind of glow.

The kids slipped inside the basement conference room and found exactly what they expected: all seven members of the Delport Instant Response Team had come together to figure out how best to respond to the blackout. It was DIRT's job to make sure the loss of electricity didn't completely stop the city. They were responsible for getting everything back up and running.

As the city planner, Ken Stevenson was in charge of keeping up to date on the scope of any emergency. When the kids arrived in the basement, he was standing in front of a map and pointing out the areas that were affected by the blackout. It covered virtually the entire region.

The phone on the conference table rang. A man pushed a button that put the call on the speaker. "This is Deputy Mayor Sirone," he said. "Who are we talking to?"

"Eric Marcolina," said the voice over the phone. "I'm the night manager at Delport Electric." Delport Electric was the company that supplied all the electricity to the area.

"What happened?" asked the fire chief. "Did we lose a transformer?"

There was a delay on the other side. "No," said Marcolina. "The transformers are all fine."

73

"Did we have a lightning hit or a line snap?" asked the deputy mayor.

"No," came the tentative voice on the other end.

"Then what went wrong?" asked Ken.

"That's the problem," said the voice. "We have no idea."

Robbie, Allen, and Josh exchanged looks. This night was getting stranger and stranger. "Berg was right," whispered Josh. "It's a government cover-up."

The DIRT members were equally confused. "What do you mean you have no idea?" asked Ken Stevenson.

"I mean we've checked everything, and we still have no idea what caused the blackout," the man answered, sounding a little defensive. "So we don't know how to fix it."

"You've got a state-of-the-art computer system," said the fire chief, "and you mean to tell me that it can't figure out why there's no power?"

"Well," said Marcolina, "the system can tell us that Power Station Three isn't producing electricity." There was a slight hesitation. "It just can't tell us why."

74

More confused looks around the table. "What are you going to do?" the deputy mayor asked.

"We've got our team working on it," said the man. There was another pause. "I'm sure they'll solve the problem in no time." His voice wasn't very convincing and the faces of the DIRT members were equally unsure.

"Okay. Keep us informed." Sirone pressed the button, cutting off the call, and turned to the others. "We'd better make sure we're ready for a long blackout. Alert the hospitals and police departments. And let's start trying to figure out what might be causing this." The DIRT members quickly scattered around the room and started working.

"Hey, kids," Ken said, coming over to them. "You might want to head on home. This looks like it's going to take a while."

Josh motioned for his father to come closer. "It's probably the CIA," he whispered conspiratorially. "You might want to place a call to Washington."

Ken just shook his head. "It's probably

75

just a computer glitch," he said. "You've got to stop watching so much TV. Anyway, do you all know where the flashlights are?"

"In the kitchen drawer," said Robbie. "Right next to the candles."

"Good," said her father. "But I don't want you using the candles until I get home. They can be dangerous."

"Gotcha," said Robbie.

An assistant came over to Ken with a giant binder marked "Delport Electric." "Here are the schematics for the entire power grid," said the assistant. "Where do you want them?"

He motioned to the table, and the assistant set the binder down with a loud thump. "I'll get out of here as soon as I can," Ken promised his kids. They looked at the binder and realized that was wishful thinking at best.

"Don't worry," his daughter told her father. "We'll be all right."

As they left the room, Robbie looked up at the map behind her father. In the center of the blacked-out zone, she saw that Power

Station 3 was located at the end of Clancy Road, not far from their house.

9:15 P.M.
NEPTUNE PARK

On their way home, the kids stopped to check out what was happening at a city park near the beach. They were surprised by what they saw. Unlike the confusion they had seen an hour earlier, people were beginning to adapt to the loss of electricity.

With no television or lights inside their homes, many people had poured out into the streets. Neighbors were talking to one another in the moonlight. Good Samaritans had taken posts at busy intersections and were directing traffic, helping to ease the flow. Some kids were dancing to music from a portable boom box on a basketball court.

"Interesting," said Allen. "People seem to be enjoying the emergency."

"It's not really that much of an emergency," said Robbie. "Nobody's in danger."

"That's because they don't know that the government cut the electricity to keep them

77

from learning the truth," said Josh. "Ignorance is bliss."

Robbie just shook her head. She knew that she and Josh were related, but sometimes she wondered if just maybe there had been a mix-up at the hospital.

"Anyway," Josh continued, "I'm going to look around for those surfer aliens. I think they have the answer to this puzzle." He quickly moved over to the crowd and started searching for Ed and Fred.

Robbie was lost in thought. It had been a busy couple of days. She still hadn't done anything to prepare for the election, and that was coming up soon. Then there was the mystery of the suddenly appearing aliens. Very strange indeed. But most of all she was worried about Erika. She had really hurt her friend's feelings, and she had no one to blame but herself.

"I'm sure you'll work it out," Allen said when she told him what was bothering her.

"I don't know," Robbie answered. "Erika's really mad. And she has every reason to be. What I did was pretty bad."

"Yes. However, you humans have a great

ability to turn a bad thing into something positive. Just look around. The loss of electricity is a great nuisance, but people have come together, and they're having a good time."

Just then Josh came running back. "Look at the horizon!"

"The Celuvians?" asked Allen.

"Better," said Josh. He pointed upward, and they saw a pair of meteorites flash across the sky. Most people called them shooting stars, but they were really rocks and other debris burning up in the atmosphere. In the past, Allen had never considered them beautiful or exciting. They were just part of the normal organization of a solar system. But out here with the crowd looking over the ocean, he saw something new in them.

At first there were just a couple of them, but they kept coming. Finally the sky was filled with a brilliant array of meteors. All of the people in the park stopped what they were doing and watched. It looked like a Fourth of July fireworks display without the loud booms.

The meteor shower continued for about

79

thirty seconds, and then it ended as suddenly as it had started. And moments later the blackout ended too.

In an instant all the lights in Delport came back on. The people in the park clapped, shook each other's hands, waved good-bye, and headed back to their homes.

"That was strange," said Josh. "It's as if the meteor shower and the blackout were related."

"I don't know what a meteorite would have to do with electricity, but it is an interesting coincidence," said Allen.

Robbie was thinking. "Maybe we'd better make a stop over at the power station."

As they hopped back on their bikes and rode off, none of them noticed the black van with the ARC 4 license plate. But inside the van, two ARC workers were compiling data from the meteor shower. Something was definitely going on.

9:48 P.M.
DELPORT ELECTRIC POWER STATION 3

The kids left their bikes at the base of a sign: Delport Electric PS3. The station consisted of three cinder-block buildings surrounded by a chain-link fence. Next to the buildings was a giant transformer that emitted a constant hum.

Someone pulled up in a Delport Electric truck and was met in the parking lot by a foreman. The kids quietly moved closer, making sure to keep out of sight. They got close enough to overhear part of the conversation.

"How'd you fix the power?" asked the man who was getting out of the truck.

"We didn't," answered the foreman. "It just came back online."

This obviously confused the truck driver. As they continued the conversation, they walked into the main building, making it impossible for the kids to hear what they were saying.

"Let's move over there," Josh suggested. He was pointing to a wooded area outside the fence. In the woods there was a clearing right next to the building. Maybe they could hear some more from that vantage point.

Robbie and Allen agreed, and the three of

them started to make their way through the woods. As they worked through the trees, they noticed a smoky odor.

"What's that smell?" Robbie asked as she walked into the clearing.

Before Allen could answer, he accidentally stepped into a puddle of green ooze. The ooze splashed onto a patch of grass, which suddenly caught fire!

CHAPTER
7

FRIDAY, 10:02 P.M.
DELPORT ELECTRIC POWER STATION 3

Josh and Robbie jumped away from the fire as it spread across the grass. Allen quickly came to the rescue, surrounding the fire with an energy field that choked off the oxygen the flames needed to burn. Still, in a matter of seconds it had left a burned patch about three feet wide.

"Be careful," Allen said as he turned to the others. "This green substance is highly flammable." Looking around, they saw globs of the green ooze on both sides of the fence. Allen used his finger to scoop up a

83

drop of it. He held it up to the moonlight to get a better look.

"What is it?" asked Robbie.

"It's a Beta fuel," he said. "It's used for long-range travel. Even small amounts can generate a lot of energy. But it's very unstable."

"What do you consider long-range?" asked Josh, who thought riding in the car for two hours to see his grandparents was an eternity.

"Six to seven light-years," Allen said matter-of-factly. He continued to examine the substance.

"When you say long," said Josh, "you mean long."

"Is it from those Celuvians?" Robbie asked. "Maybe this is where they landed."

"No," Allen replied. "This is definitely Pontine. The Pontines are from the Nosyarg galaxy. Unlike the Celuvians, they are advanced. Very advanced." He looked around the clearing. There were some broken branches and a couple of other patches of burned grass. "They've been here, but they're gone now."

"That makes two different alien species landing near Delport at around the same time," Josh said.

"There *is* a significant amount of alien activity going on," Allen agreed as he used an energy field to safely burn off the rest of the fuel. "I just wish I knew why."

SATURDAY, 9:45 A.M.
THE STEVENSON HOUSE

"Unbelievable," Josh said as he scanned the morning newspaper. He read a portion of an article to Robbie and Allen: "'According to Eric Marcolina of Delport Electric, the blackout was a direct result of the Carbon Canyon earthquake on Thursday.

"'Marcolina said that the tremors loosened transistor connections in the main computer, causing a relay to malfunction.'" Josh looked at them as though what he had read was extremely scandalous. "Can you believe this?"

"Yes," said Robbie. "It sounds totally reasonable."

"Of course it does," replied her younger brother. "Unless, of course, you take into

85

account the alien ooze that Allen discovered at the power station. Then it doesn't sound reasonable at all."

"Good point," said Allen.

"Or the Celuvians we saw in Carbon Canyon," Josh added. "Something weird is definitely going on here."

"You might be right," said Allen. "I've been thinking about it. The Celuvians are from the Chronos galaxy, which is way over here." As he talked, a three-dimensional map of the universe appeared like a hologram before them. A red light started whirling to mark the Chronos galaxy.

"And the Pontines are from the Nosyarg galaxy over here." A blue light swirled, signifying the Nosyarg galaxy. It's a massive statistical improbability that they'd both wind up at about the same location on Earth at approximately the same time *by accident.*"

Robbie looked down at a map lying on the kitchen table. It was the one her father had used at the DIRT meeting the night before. "Well, we know that the Pontines were here," she said as she put a penny at the end of Clancy Road, where the power station was located.

"And we saw the Celuvians over here," added Allen, putting a penny on Carbon Canyon. "And since they had taken the appearance of surfers, we can assume that the first place they visited was the beach." Allen put a third penny down at the beach.

"But what does it mean?" asked Robbie.

"I have no idea," said Allen. "It's improbable that this is a coincidence, but I guess it's technically not impossible."

"Yes, it is," said Josh with a sudden burst of excitement. "Look at the map. It's just like the monument beacons on *Watch the Skies*."

"What?" said Allen.

"The three points," said Josh. "They all line up."

Robbie and Allen looked down and saw that Josh was right. The pennies marking the locations of the three sightings were all in a straight line on the map.

Josh continued. "And they're pointing right here." His finger traced along the imaginary line and came to a stop. "Pacific Point."

87

Now a light went on for Robbie. "Which is where the waves are suddenly so high." Robbie was beginning to believe in Josh's theory. "Okay, Josh. I think you may be right. Something is going on here."

An idea occurred to Allen. "They might be tags," he said.

"What are tags?" asked Josh.

"Whenever different species plan to meet on a third planet, they tag the meeting place with various types of energy so that everyone can find the location. Kind of like putting out a welcome sign."

"So the Celuvians and the Pontines are going to have a big party here in Delport," said Josh, getting excited. "And these guys are just like the decorating committee getting ready for it."

"Not quite," said Allen. "The Celuvians and Pontines don't do anything together. Their home planets are extremely far apart and they have no shared interests. There's no reason for the two of them to meet unless they're part of something much bigger."

The thought of something "much bigger" interested Josh. "Like what?"

"Like an Intergalactic Congress," said Allen. "It's a meeting of species from throughout the universe. Kind of like the United Nations, but for planets and galaxies."

Josh could barely contain himself. "You mean aliens from all over the universe are coming to Delport?"

"It's a possibility," said Allen.

"It'll be like a *Star Trek* convention!" Josh exclaimed. "Except the people will really be from different galaxies. And we'll have front-row seats!"

Something about Allen's demeanor let Robbie know he was thinking about something else—something more important than Josh's excitement about an alien convention. And she thought she knew what it was. "If it's an Intergalactic Congress," she said, "there might be a representative from Xela."

Allen just looked at her and nodded. That was exactly what he had been thinking. Ever since he was accidentally stranded on Earth, Allen had been trying to get word of his location back to his home planet. Although

he loved being with Robbie and Josh and learning about Earth, he longed to return to Xela. Now he might have a chance.

Allen rushed up to the Stevensons' attic, which had become his home away from home.

"What are you looking for?" asked Josh, following him.

"I made a beacon," he said. "I've never used it because it's not strong enough to transmit beyond your solar system."

"But if any Xelans come into our solar system, they would be able to detect it," Robbie finished, joining them.

"Exactly," said Allen. He was trying not to get too excited. He still wasn't certain that an Intergalactic Congress was about to occur, but it seemed like a reasonable assumption.

The beacon was an egg-shaped green crystal about eight inches tall. "Here it is," he said as he showed it to them. "It pulsates, emitting a sound wave that is specific to Xelan communication."

"How does it work?" Josh asked.

"It's all powered by this." He held up the

crystal, but his words trailed off as something about the beacon caught his eye. His smile suddenly disappeared.

"What's the matter?" asked Robbie.

"The energy source," Allen said turning the crystal to show her a small crack in its surface. "It's ruined. It must have been damaged during the earthquake."

Allen was distraught. Robbie didn't know how to comfort him.

"This is bad, huh?" she offered.

"Very bad," he said.

Then a smile came over her face. "Then it's a good thing we humans are so good at turning a bad thing into something positive."

Allen looked at her in confusion.

"We can fix it," she said. "I don't know how. But I know we can."

"Definitely," added Josh.

Allen smiled.

SATURDAY, 1:20 P.M.
DELPORT HIGH SCHOOL

The problem of powering Allen's beacon was that it couldn't exactly be plugged into

a wall socket. They needed to find an alternative source of power. Although Allen was made of energy, he couldn't power it. His strength fluctuated throughout the day. The fluctuation would distort the transmission, making the beacon useless. For the beacon to work, it needed a steady source of energy that could last for days.

They couldn't run it off of a battery because there was no way to thread a wire from the battery into the crystal, which was one solid piece. In the midst of their frustration, Robbie remembered a physics experiment.

In science class, she had seen a demonstration of a device called a Tesla coil. The coil was a type of electromagnet that produced a field of energy. She figured that if they slipped the tip of the crystal into the coil, the coil could power the beacon. Unfortunately, the only Tesla coil she knew of was locked in a cabinet in Mr. Cavanaugh's lab. That was why Robbie and Allen had come to the school.

Sneaking into the school wasn't something Robbie would normally have done, but the Tesla coil was the only thing that could help Allen get home. She could just imagine the headlines: "Candidate for Class President Caught Breaking into School." N one would believe her reason for doing it.

Getting past the locked doors was easy for Allen. Although he appeared to be a normal teenager, he was an alien who could transform himself into his natural blue energy form and pass through solid objects. Once he was inside the school, he opened the door and let Robbie in.

It was odd to be in the school with no one else around. The building was deserted, and their every step echoed down the hallways. Robbie noticed an Angie Gordon campaign poster, which reminded her that she still hadn't done any campaigning for the election.

The door to the physics lab was also locked, so Allen once again transformed himself into his energy form and let Robbie in. There was a danger in these transformations. They weakened him. Transforming himself over and over again had a profound effect on his energy level. Still, the result

93

could be worth the risk. He had a chance to get word back to Xela.

Allen and Robbie found the Tesla coil in a closet and placed it on the demonstration table. Allen pulled the crystal from his pocket and slipped it right inside the coil.

"Perfect," he said. He was genuinely excited. "This should work."

They left the lab and headed for the exit. But this time the school wasn't quiet. This time they were alarmed by a noise.

At first Robbie and Allen heard scratching. Then they heard rapid breathing. But by the time they realized what was happening, it was too late.

The Doberman pinscher turned the corner and kept a close eye on Allen and Robbie. The dog barked a few times, the sound echoing through the school. The presence of the Doberman meant that the security guard couldn't be far away, and the dog was blocking the exit.

"What do we do?" whispered Allen.

"We can't get to the exit," said Robbie.

The dog started walking toward them slowly.

"We better go back into the physics lab," she continued. "Maybe we can make it to the rear exit."

Allen reached for the doorknob. But the door had locked automatically. He quickly switched into his blue energy form so that he could pass back through. But his energy level was so low that he couldn't force his way through.

While this was going on, the dog continued toward them.

Faced with no better option, Robbie came up with a plan. "Run!" she said. The two kids tore off in the opposite direction from the dog and raced toward the maze of lockers in the middle of the school.

It had taken Robbie half a semester to learn her way through these; maybe they could lose the dog. They separated and quietly tried to hurry down different aisles. The watchdog reached the maze and started sniffing.

"Allen," Robbie whispered when she saw her friend emerge from one aisle. "Over here."

She had slipped out of view behind a large

drinking fountain. Allen crawled over to her and they pressed their backs against the wall. They waited for what seemed to be a few minutes without hearing anything.

"Think we lost him?" whispered Allen.

Robbie didn't even answer. The low growl from the other side of the water fountain told them everything they needed to know.

CHAPTER 8

SATURDAY, 1:55 P.M.
DELPORT HIGH SCHOOL

The Doberman's teeth were just inches away from Allen's face. Its growl was frightening, but even worse were its sporadic barks, especially when they finally attracted the attention of the security guard.

"Whatcha got, boy?" the guard yelled from a distant hallway. He would be there in seconds.

Allen reached out and placed his hand on the dog's head. Xelans were the great communicators of the galaxy, and Allen could

97

communicate with this dog just as easily as he was able to talk to Robbie and Josh. After a few moments the dog turned around and raced in the opposite direction.

Robbie and Allen remained hidden until the security guard rushed past them. "I'm coming!" he yelled as he followed the dog toward the cafeteria. "I'm coming."

"How did you do that?" asked Robbie.

"I just told the dog where they store the hamburger meat," Allen said with a smile. "Now let's get out of here."

4:20 P.M.
DELPORT ELECTRIC POWER STATION 3

The operatives from the ARC van were carefully collecting samples from the burned spots in the clearing next to the power station. Unlike Robbie, Allen, and Josh the night before, the operatives wore protective gloves and goggles. They scooped up the burned remains of the green ooze with a long metal spoon and poured it into a stainless-steel test tube.

7:40 p.m.
PACIFIC POINT

As the sky grew dark, Allen, Robbie, and Josh headed for the beach to set up the beacon. To ensure that his message was heard, Allen wanted to place it at the location where the Intergalactic Congress was to take place. He figured Pacific Point was his spot.

On the map, all the signs indicated the Point. Also, the large waves happened before the earthquake or the blackout, meaning it was probably the first and most important of the tags. But most of all, it made sense to hold the congress on the beach so that creatures from liquid-based planets could congregate in the water and those from solid based ones could congregate on the sand.

The kids found the perfect spot for the beacon atop a lifeguard hut. The hut was set on a platform that provided lifeguards with a bird's-eye view of the beach. Putting the beacon there would keep it high and out of most people's way. Most important, the hut had an outdoor power outlet.

Robbie plugged in the Tesla coil and placed it on the roof of the hut. Allen then carefully slipped the crystal beacon into the coil. After a few moments, it started to emit a light green glow.

"It's working," Allen said with a smile. "It's transmitting."

The three of them were pleased. The beacon was in the perfect spot. It was hidden from view and would go unnoticed. No one would know it was there, except the three of them and the Xelan who picked up its message.

They sat down on the beach and watched the sun during its final moments before setting. The sunset was a stunning array of orange and purple streaks across the sky. The clouds and the whitecaps on the ocean combined to make the view perfect.

"I was reading a book on photography," Robbie said. "And it said this time of day is known as the magic hour because of all the brilliant colors in the sky."

"It's well named," said Allen. "I've never seen anything as beautiful as Earth sunsets."

They enjoyed the scene for a moment

more, and then Robbie looked at Allen. "I hope this is one of the last sunsets you see."

At first Allen didn't know what she meant, but then he figured it out. If the beacon worked, he'd be heading home to Xela in just a matter of days. That was great, but it was also sad. It meant he would never see Robbie and Josh again.

"Just in case it is," Allen replied, "let's make sure to enjoy it all."

No one said a word as they sat and watched the last colors fade from the horizon.

SUNDAY, 1:30 P.M.
FLAVIA'S PIZZERIA

Sunday morning was filled with chores at the Stevenson house. Because Ken had been called away to DIRT meetings on back-to-back nights that week, they were even further behind schedule than usual. Robbie did laundry, Allen washed and dried the dishes, and Josh worked in the yard. Then they all picked up around the house. To show his appreciation, Ken took them all out for lunch.

"How's the election campaign going?" Ken asked his daughter.

"I haven't done much campaigning," said Robbie. "I haven't had a lot of free time."

"You'd better hurry," said Allen. "The election's at the end of next week. You still need to write your speech, make signs, and figure out your platform."

"You're my campaign manager," Robbie protested. "You're supposed to be assisting me. Aren't you going to help me come up with a campaign strategy?"

"I've been thinking about that," said Allen. "According to everything I've read, the key to getting elected seems to be appealing to special interest groups. You know, like the athletes or the surfer kids."

"I still can't believe you guys are doing this," said Josh. "All government is corrupt."

Ken Stevenson couldn't believe his ears. "How can you say that?" he asked. "*I* work for the government."

"I've read all about it, Dad," said Josh.

"Well," countered his father. "you can't

believe everything you come across on the Internet."

"What about Watergate and Teapot Dome and all those other political scandals?" Josh asked. "Aren't those real?"

"Yes," said Ken. "But our government has also done a lot of great things, like public schools and highways"—an idea came to him—"and putting a man on the moon. Think about that. The government has placed twelve different men on the moon and that's a quarter of a million miles away."

Allen couldn't help smiling. The moon was just next door compared to the millions of miles he had traveled from Xela. Still, he agreed with Mr. Stevenson. "I think you're right," he said. "I think government can do really great things. And I think Robbie would make a fantastic class president."

"You keep saying that," she replied. "But I still don't see how I can get elected. Losing is okay. You've got to accept that possibility."

"I know," Ken said, holding up a slice of

pizza with everything on it. "You should run your campaign on the pizza platform."

Everyone looked at him curiously. "What's the pizza platform?" Robbie asked warily.

"Your campaign should be like this pizza," he said. "It has a little bit of everything, just like you. Let the other candidates appeal to the special interest groups and run dull cheese-and-pepperoni campaigns. You need to reach out to everybody. You need to be a Flavia's Super Supreme"

"I like it," said Allen. "The Pizza Platform."

7:45 P.M.
THE STEVENSON HOUSE
Robbie and Allen had spent the rest of the day working on her new pizza campaign. They made round signs that looked like pizzas with slogans like "Stevenson, a candidate with everything on top" and "Vote for Robbie, She Delivers."

Robbie was even working on a speech with a pizza theme. It was funny and got to the point. She talked about how all pizzas were not alike, just as all candidates were not alike. She was straight from the oven, and the others were all frozen.

They continued to work into the night. Even Josh started to help. "I guess if someone's going to be class president," he said as explanation, "I'd rather it be my sister."

CHAPTER
9

MONDAY, 7:50 A.M.
DELPORT HIGH SCHOOL

As they walked into the school, Robbie began to worry that the watchdog was still looking for her. This, despite the fact that the school was open and filled with bleary-eyed students starting the week.

Robbie and Allen had come early to put her campaign posters up. They placed them in busiest parts of school so that more people would see them. But the walls were getting crowded with posters for the candidates for all the offices.

Robbie was putting up one of her pizza

posters when she saw Erika. It was the first time she had seen her friend since upsetting her at lunch the previous Friday.

"Hey, Erika," Robbie said awkwardly. "How's it going?"

"Good," Erika replied. "Very good."

"I tried to reach you this weekend, but you were never home," Robbie replied.

"I was busy," Erika said curtly. "Timmy and I were working on our campaign."

"Good," said Robbie. "I'm sure it'll go great." She knew it would take a while before Erika forgave her, but she would make sure that it did eventually happen.

Allen, meanwhile, was in the library watching an impromptu debate between Timmy and Mike Archer.

"If I'm elected," Mike said, "I guarantee less homework, fewer classes, and better lunches."

This brought a big cheer from the crowd that had formed. Allen couldn't believe it. He knew that a student couldn't have any impact on such matters. Certainly the other kids knew it, too. But they didn't care. They were cheering for Mike anyway.

107

"If I'm elected," said Timmy, "I'm going to work with the library to get a computer with Internet access for students doing research. And I'm going to start a recycling program. It's good for the environment, and it will help raise money for school activities."

Allen liked Timmy's ideas, but the other students, led by Mike, just laughed at him. "Go back to the chess club," said one sophomore.

"I think your ideas are great," Allen said as a dejected Timmy walked past him.

"Really?" Timmy said. "Do you mean that?"

"Absolutely," said Allen.

"Does that mean you'll vote for me?" Timmy asked. There was a hint of excitement in his voice.

"I can't, really," said Allen. "I'm Robbie's campaign manager. I have to vote for her."

This seemed to depress Timmy even more. "Oh, well," he said, "thanks for liking my ideas."

Allen felt sad as he watched Tim walk away. It didn't seem fair. Mike Archer and

Angie Gordon, who didn't have any ideas at all, were in the lead simply because they were popular. Meanwhile Timmy and Robbie, who would do a great job, were way behind.

Maybe Josh was right, Allen said to himself. *Maybe all government is corrupt.*

Allen went into the library and speed-read some more books on American history. This time he picked out all the stories of government corruption, the kinds of stories that Josh had talked about at the pizza parlor. He read about bribery and bugging, spying and voter fraud. It was almost more than he could take.

"Allen?" Robbie was tapping him on the shoulder. "Allen? Are you okay?"

"Yes," Allen answered. "I'm just a little disappointed. I've been reading these books, and Josh is right. Government really *is* corrupt."

"Governments have problems, like all other institutions," Robbie said. "But they also do a lot of good things, as my father said."

"But Mike or Angie will probably win the

109

election," he said. "Even though you'd do a better job."

"I've always thought one of them would win," she replied.

"Maybe we should cheat," he said. Robbie couldn't believe what she was hearing. "You would be a better president," he reasoned, "so you should win. And with my powers I can make sure you win this election."

"That's ridiculous," she said. "Just because some people are corrupt doesn't mean you or I should be. As long as most people keep being honest and fair, democracy's got a chance of working out right."

From the library they went to Mr. Tyree's history class. Before the lecture started, Mr. Tyree made an announcement.

"I'm sure we're all looking forward to sixth period so that we can hear what Ms. Stevenson has to say," the teacher said from the front of the room.

Robbie had absolutely no idea what he was talking about. "What do you mean?" she asked.

"Don't be silly," he said. "Sixth period.

That's when all the candidates are giving their speeches at the class assembly.

The color instantly drained from Robbie's face. "Speeches?" she said pointedly to Allen. "Today?"

"Didn't I tell you?" Allen asked sheepishly.

1:15 P.M.
PACIFIC POINT

The black ARC van had returned to Pacific Point. But this time the operatives weren't checking the waves. This time they were studying a transmission they had picked up with some of their equipment. A pulsing sound wave was emanating from the beach. They didn't know it, but it was Allen's beacon.

The two ARC operatives walked along the beach with a device that looked like a metal detector except that it beeped faster as they got closer to Allen's crystal. It only took them ten minutes to determine that the transmission was coming from the lifeguard hut.

The first operative scrambled up to where Robbie and Allen had climbed two days ear-

111

lier. He unplugged the Tesla coil and then took both it and the crystal down from the roof of the hut.

They both carefully examined the crystal, taking care not to destroy any latent fingerprints. They didn't know what to make of the crystal or how to trace its origin. It would be taken to the primary ARC lab for analysis. The Tesla coil, though, was a different matter. On the base of the coil was an interesting label: Property of Delport High School.

The second operative pulled a cell phone out of his pocket and hit the button to automatically call headquarters.

"I think we've got something here," he said into the phone. "Something big."

2:15 P.M.
DELPORT HIGH SCHOOL

As the auditorium filled with students, Robbie paced nervously backstage. She had worked on a speech, but it was nowhere near finished. She had thought she had a couple of days before she was to deliver it. She'd have to wing it and hope Mr. Tyree was right when he said she was a natural public speaker.

Mike Archer and Angie Gordon sat back confidently as though they had done this a million times. Timmy Ryan, though, was nervous. He didn't like getting up in front of large crowds, especially because he knew they might taunt him. Still, he had a great speech filled with good ideas. Listening to him practice it, Robbie was impressed. She began to think that Timmy might do all right for himself. She didn't believe he would be elected, but she thought he might win some voters over.

Of course, Robbie was mostly thinking about the fact that she was about to do one of her least favorite things—speak in front of a large group of people. She didn't know why she hated it so much; she just did. To make matters worse, the candidates were speaking in alphabetical order. That meant she would be last, dragging the agony out even longer.

Mike Archer got up first. He was instantly greeted with a wave of applause. His speech was good, filled with smart ideas and a couple of jokes. The audience loved it.

113

It was Timmy's speech!

Mike had heard Timmy practicing and had stolen most of the best stuff. Robbie couldn't believe it. She had never known Mike very well, but she'd always assumed that he was a nice guy. She had certainly never imagined that he would steal a speech. As Mike returned to his seat, he gave Timmy a wink and said, "Thanks for the help."

Robbie was furious. She was so mad that she momentarily forgot about her nervousness.

Angie Gordon followed. She had a little difficulty with her speech. She was obviously nervous, and her words ran together. Instead of saying, "Fellow students, ask not what Delport can do for you but what you can do for Delport," she said, "Fellow studentsasknotwhatDelportcandoforyou." The speech itself was over in less than thirty seconds.

Angie's difficulty made Robbie nervous again. She had figured that Angie would be a natural at public speaking. She began to think that her speech might go just as badly.

First, though, Timmy Ryan had to give his speech—or, rather, his new speech. He didn't want to repeat the parts that Mike had used because people would think he had stolen the ideas from Mike.

He started a little slowly but picked up speed. He wasn't as confident as Mike had been, but the speech was still pretty good. In fact, his new speech was even better than the first one. Robbie was amazed that he managed to pull it off. Better yet, she was encouraged by the applause that followed it. It wasn't loud, but it was sincere.

Then it dawned on her. That applause meant it was her turn to speak. Robbie's heart started to race as Mr. Tyree called her to the lectern.

She looked out at the auditorium filled with students and knew there was no way out. She cleared her throat and adjusted the microphone. It seemed like forever before she took control of her fear and got started.

"My name is Robbie Stevenson and I really like pizza," she said. Much to her surprise, some people laughed. Maybe this wouldn't be so bad.

115

"In fact, I like pizza so much that I'm running my campaign on it." She looked over at Allen and he flashed her a big smile. "If you ask me, the best pizza in town is over at Flavia's." Some people in the crowd agreed and showed it with a little applause.

"These days Flavia's is always crowded. But when it first opened, no one went there. It didn't look as stylish as the bigger pizza places. And it didn't have catchy commercials. It just had great pizza." More crowd reaction. "It makes me think of Timmy."

The crowd quieted for a moment, unsure where she was going. But Robbie now knew exactly what she wanted to say.

"Timmy is a lot like Flavia's," she continued. "He may not be as flashy as the other places, but he makes the best pizza. My mother told me that when something is really good, people have a way of finding out about it.

"Everybody found out about Flavia's, and I think everyone will find out about Timmy. That's why I would like to withdraw from the race and ask you all to vote for Timmy

Ryan. I think he'll be a great class president."

After a few moments of stunned silence, the crowd applauded. In fact, just about the only one who didn't clap was Timmy. He was too surprised. As Robbie returned to her seat, she smiled at Timmy and then looked over at Mike. She gave him a mischievous wink just like the one he had given Timmy a few minutes earlier.

117

CHAPTER 10

"I don't understand," Allen said to Robbie in the hall outside the auditorium. "Your speech was terrific. You had a real chance to win. And you gave it all away."

"Sounds like you understand perfectly," Robbie answered.

"But why?" Allen was dumbfounded. "I know that you wanted to be class president. Why would you give it up?"

"Timmy will do a better job than I would have done," said Robbie. "You wanted to learn about democracy. Well, in a democracy you have to make some sacrifices for the greater good. I would have enjoyed being class president. But Timmy will make school better for more people."

"Every time I think I understand you," Allen said. "I find out something new."

"That's good," said Robbie. "After all, you're supposed to be learning while you're here."

Timmy and Erika came over to Robbie. "That was really great how you stood up for me," Timmy said. "I don't know how to thank you."

"That's easy," she said. "If you win the election, do a good job."

"Absolutely," said Timmy.

He flashed her another smile and walked away.

Erika hung back, unsure of how to break the awkward silence between her and Robbie. "I'm really sorry" both girls blurted out at the same time.

Robbie laughed. "I really *am* sorry, Erika. When you first mentioned being my campaign manager, I should have explained that it was Allen's idea for me to run for office."

119

"And maybe I *am* a little too sensitive," Erika added.

"Just a little," Robbie agreed with a wink. "I'm just glad I didn't do any permanent damage to our friendship."

As Erika left to rejoin Timmy, Robbie smiled to think that things were back to normal between her and Erika. Her happy mood was broken, though, when she looked through the window and saw the ARC van in the teachers' parking lot.

"What are they doing here?" Robbie asked.

"I don't know," Allen said. "But I don't think this is a good sign."

They turned the corner and looked down the hall. There they saw a team of ARC operatives standing outside Mr. Cavanaugh's classroom.

"The Tesla coil," said Robbie. "They must have found it."

The operatives were holding electronic devices much more advanced than the ones Phil Berg had used in Carbon Canyon. One of the devices started to emit low beeps.

"There's some residue over here," said the ARC agent with the beeping meter. He was holding the meter up against the door that Allen had passed through. Allen was certain that they were measuring some part of his energy.

"We'd better clear out of here," he said to Robbie. "I don't want them getting that thing close to me."

7:00 P.M.
PACIFIC POINT

Although Robbie and Allen were pretty certain they knew what had happened, they went back to the lifeguard hut with Josh to check for the crystal. It was nowhere to be seen.

"I'm so sorry," said Robbie. "But maybe it got the message out before they found it. Maybe the Xelan delegate has already arrived for the Intergalactic Congress."

"Maybe," Allen replied. "I can always hope."

"Check it out," Josh said, pointing down the beach. "There's Phil Berg."

121

Once again, Berg was planning to do a remote broadcast. He was going to do his show from the beach. They walked over to where he was setting up.

"Why are you broadcasting from down here?" Josh asked one of the technicians.

"He's convinced there's going to be some big alien landing tonight," said the man, as he lugged equipment through the sand.

"Do you think he knows something?" whispered Robbie.

"I'm telling you," Josh said. "He's a smart guy. Maybe that Intergalactic Congress is meeting tonight."

"I think you're right," said Allen.

"You do?" said Josh. "Because of Phil Berg?"

"No," he answered. "Because of *them*." He pointed to the parking lot. The ARC vans had arrived.

7:30 P.M.
KOONTZ NAVAL AIR STATION

The ARC agent looked over the shoulder of the radar man in the control tower overlooking the airfield. A single bleep went out periodically as the radar arm swiped across the empty screen. Then, in an instant, the screen was filled with green blips converging on Pacific Point. Then they were gone. This pattern continued to repeat itself.

"How long has this been going on?" asked the agent.

"For about thirty minutes," the radar man replied. "We have no idea what's causing it. We sent a jet over there, but the pilot didn't see a thing."

"It must be some sort of weather disturbance," said the man from ARC.

"Believe me," said the radar man, "that is no weather disturbance."

The ARC agent just smiled. "Well, that's what the report will say."

Down on the airstrip, four navy pilots were starting up their Apache helicopters. In near silence the choppers rose from the pad and moved out in perfect formation.

"Roger that," one pilot said into his microphone. "We are clear for rendezvous two miles north of Pacific Point."

7:50 P.M.
PACIFIC POINT

"This is great," Robbie said. "If they're coming tonight, you'll be here. You'll be able to contact the Xelan representative."

"You're right," said Allen. "It doesn't matter about the beacon. I'll be right here."

"I still don't know why they'd pick Earth for their meeting place," Josh said.

Allen tried to think of an explanation. "You know that Woodstock concert?"

"Back in the sixties, right?" said Robbie.

"They held it on some unused farmland," said Allen. "That way it wouldn't make a difference if they messed it up some."

"Hey," an offended Josh protested. "We're not just some abandoned old piece of dirt. We've got feelings down here on Earth."

"I was just kidding," said Allen. "They probably picked this beach because you humans have a good reputation throughout the galaxies."

Robbie and Josh smiled. That answer sounded all right to them.

The kids were sitting at the front of the crowd getting ready to see the taping of

Watch the Skies. Just as Berg was about to go on the air, another meteor shower lit up the sky over the ocean. This one was even more intense than the earlier one. The meteorites seemed to be plunging into the ocean, which had a faint glow to it.

"Are those aliens?" Josh asked.

"Not yet," said Allen. "They're more like headlights shining in front of a car. But the first wave of delegates must be pretty close."

"Quick, quick," Berg yelled. "Power up. Let's get on the air with this."

This time Berg's director didn't waste a second. She got the broadcast up and on the air.

"Good evening and welcome to *Watch the Skies,*" said Berg. "I am standing on the beach at Pacific Point. If you look out over the water you will see some unexplained lights."

Berg was getting into it. He was excited. Then he noticed that the light on the camera wasn't on anymore.

"Not another blackout," he barked.

But there was power everywhere else. This

125

loss of power was the handiwork of ARC. They had pulled the plug on Berg's show.

"You will not be allowed to transmit from this area," an ARC official shouted through a loudspeaker. "This is a military zone and must be cleared of all civilians. You must exit the beach immediately."

"Military zone?" Allen said. "What is he talking about?"

The kids looked out and saw a fleet of helicopters up ahead. A wave of uniformed soldiers was marching down the beach toward them.

ARC was moving in for a confrontation with the aliens. "We've got to stop this," said Allen. He couldn't help feeling somewhat responsible. His beacon had helped the agency determine the landing site. Now the alien delegates were in jeopardy.

"How?" asked Josh. "It's not like you can tell the ARC to go away."

"I know," said Allen, "but we've got to think of something."

"Maybe we can warn the delegates," suggested Robbie.

"If only my beacon wasn't broken," said Allen.

The glow in the water intensified. They were quickly running out of time.

"Get away from my truck!" Phil Berg was shouting at a group of ARC agents approaching his production vehicle.

"The truck!" Allen pointed at the large satellite dish on the roof. "If I can get into that truck, I can send a universal alert signal."

"Good luck," said Josh, looking at the crowd of security guards now surrounding the vehicle. "You've got a better chance of building a new beacon."

"Come on," Robbie said to Josh. "We can buy Allen some time."

"How are we going to do that?" asked Josh.

Robbie looked down and saw a discarded tube of suntan lotion lying on the ground. "Just follow my lead."

The ARC commander was still arguing with Berg when Robbie and Josh came running up.

127

"There are aliens down there," Robbie said pointing down the beach.

"What's that on your face?" asked Berg.

Both of the kids had large globs of suntan lotion on their cheeks.

"It's some sort of slime," said Josh. "It shot out of their eye sockets."

The combination of their gross description and the general panic on the beach was enough to distract Berg and the ARC commander while Allen turned into his blue energy form and slipped through the wall of the truck.

"Now what?" he asked himself as he looked at the high-tech equipment that filled the vehicle. He searched through a file cabinet and found a packet of manuals. Within seconds, Allen knew how to operate every piece of equipment in front of him.

Through the window he could see the glow of the approaching delegations. At the speed they were likely traveling, they wouldn't notice the military presence on the beach until it was too late. Allen knew that he was their only hope.

He hacked his way into the computer and started typing in some coordinates for the satellite dish. Above him, he heard the dish move on the roof. No longer was it facing Delport. He was aiming for a point out over the water. Allen felt this would give him the best chance to reach the arriving delegates.

He began to relax as he typed a universal alert code into the computer. But just as he was about to send it, something happened. The truck moved.

It was Phil Berg. He had managed to force his way into the cab and was trying to outrun the ARC agents.

"Stop the truck immediately," Allen heard someone shout over a bullhorn outside.

Berg ignored the order. He was going to find a spot and get back on the air.

According to the manuals, the satellite dish couldn't transmit while the truck was moving. Allen's message couldn't get out unless he was able to stop it.

Thunder crackled outside and the sky had a purple glow. The delegates would be there

in seconds. Allen could think of only one way to stop Berg.

Allen stretched his face until it was twice its normal size and then leaned through the door to the truck's cabin. When Berg saw Allen's reflection in his rearview mirror he let out a scream and slammed on the brakes.

The moment the truck stopped, Allen sent the alert signal and returned to his blue energy form. While a tongue-tied Berg tried to say something, Allen passed right back through the truck's wall and disappeared.

10:00 P.M.
THE STEVENSON HOUSE

Using the telescope in the attic, Allen was able to see the space traffic as the delegates bypassed Earth and continued on to the far reaches of the solar system.

ARC and Phil Berg would wait at the beach for days before giving up, but Allen knew that the delegates to the Intergalactic Congress would never arrive. His message had reached them. He had saved the day, but he had paid a high price for doing so.

Not only did he miss his chance to search for the Xelan delegate, but his warning virtually ensured that such a gathering would not be scheduled to take place on Earth again.

"Why'd you do it?" Robbie asked as they took turns looking into the night sky.

"Democracy," he said. "It means putting the needs of many ahead of the needs of one."

Robbie just looked at him and smiled.

"I'm glad you're my friend, Allen."

"Me too," he responded.

ALIEN FACT FILE

Celuvos

Location: Chronos Galaxy

Inhabitants: Celuvians are energy-based life-forms known throughout the galaxy as "mirror creatures" because they can perfectly mimic any species they encounter.

Average Celuvian life span: 100 Celvoids (60 Earth years)

Number of Celuvians on Celuvos: 1,138. Few Celuvians remain on Celuvos. They are explorers by nature, and most travel in pairs on lifelong journeys throughout the universe.

Number of Celuvians on Earth: 2 confirmed, although as many as 100 Celuvians are thought to have assimilated into everyday Earth life.

Celuvian Games: Because they travel in pairs, Celuvians are avid game players. Their favorites include Niise, which is like marbles, and Melpud, which is similar to chess.

Celuvian weaknesses: Although they are great mimics, Celuvians aren't great at understanding the creatures they impersonate. They can use words, for example, but they have a difficult time forming sentences that make sense.

Scientific advances: As they travel from planet to planet, Celuvians carry scientific concepts from one solar system to another. For example, they played a crucial role in the development of the clock on Earth. (Chronos, the name of their galaxy, is also the Greek word for time.)

Interesting fact: Because Celuvians travel so extensively, they are the official scouts of the Intergalactic Congress. It is their job to locate and secure meeting areas for any congressional forums.

ARC Alien File reference #: 1737

Josh Stevenson's Alien File #: 006

About the Author

JAMES PONTI lives in Winter Park, Florida, with his wife, Denise, and his sons, Alex and Grayson. Growing up in Florida, Ponti first became interested in interplanetary travel during trips to the Kennedy Space Center, where he would watch Apollo and space shuttle launches. He has written for numerous television shows for Nickelodeon, the Disney Channel, and ABC. Currently he is the producer of the show *Roller Jam*. This is his sixth book.